Annie stepped aside so Jack could look out of the window too.

"Oh, wow," he said. What he saw took his breath away.

He stared at a rocky grey land. The land was filled with giant craters and tall mountains. The sun was shining. But the sky was ink-black!

"Say hi to the moon," Annie said softly.

Read all the adventures of
Jack and *Annie*!

Magic Tree House™

MOON MISSION!

MARY POPE OSBORNE

Illustrated by Philippe Masson

RED FOX

MOON MISSION!
A RED FOX BOOK 978 1 862 30569 4

Published in Great Britain by Red Fox,
an imprint of Random House Children's Books
A Random House Group Company

Published in the US, as *Midnight on the Moon*,
by Random House Children's Books, a division of Random House Inc, 1996

Red Fox edition published 2008

1 3 5 7 9 10 8 6 4 2

The Random House Group Limited makes every effort to ensure that the papers
used in its books are made from trees that have been legally sourced from well-
managed and credibly certified forests. Our paper procurement policy can be
found at: www.randomhouse.co.uk/paper.htm

Set in 16/21pt Bembo MT Schoolbook by
Falcon Oast Graphic Art Ltd.

Red Fox Books are published by Random House Children's Books,
61–63 Uxbridge Road, London W5 5SA

www.kidsatrandomhouse.com
www.rbooks.co.uk

Addresses for companies within The Random House Group Limited can be found
at: www.randomhouse.co.uk/offices.htm

THE RANDOM HOUSE GROUP Limited Reg. No. 954009

A CIP catalogue record for this book is available from the British Library.

Printed in the UK by CPI Bookmarque, Croydon, CR0 4TD

*For Jacob and Elena Levi and
Aram and Molly Hanessian*

Contents

Prologue

One summer day in Frog Valley a mysterious tree house appeared in the woods.

Eight-year-old Jack and his seven-year-old sister, Annie, climbed into the tree house.

The tree house was filled with books and it was *magic*. It could go any place that was in a book. All Jack and Annie had to do was point to a picture and wish to go there.

They visited dinosaurs, knights, an

Egyptian queen, pirates, ninjas and the Amazon rainforest.

Along the way, they discovered that the tree house belonged to Morgan le Fay. Morgan was a magical librarian from the time of King Arthur. She travelled through time and space, gathering books for her library.

One day, Jack and Annie found a note that said Morgan was under a spell. They set out in the magic tree house to find four special things that would free her.

With the help of a mouse named Peanut, Jack and Annie found the first thing in ancient Japan, the second in the Amazon rainforest and the third in the Ice Age.

Now Jack, Annie and Peanut are ready to find the last thing . . . in *Moon Mission!*

1

By Moonlight

"Jack!" whispered a voice.

Jack opened his eyes. He saw a figure in the moonlight.

"Wake up. Get dressed." It was his sister, Annie.

Jack turned on his light. He rubbed his eyes.

Annie was standing beside his bed. She wore jeans and a sweatshirt.

"Let's go to the tree house," she said.

"What time is it?" asked Jack. He put on his glasses.

3

"Don't look at your clock," said Annie.

Jack looked at his clock. "Oh, no," he said. "It's midnight. It's too dark."

"No, it isn't. The moon makes it bright enough to see," said Annie.

"Wait till the morning," said Jack.

"No. Now," said Annie. "We have to find the fourth M thing. I have a feeling that the full moon might help us."

"That's crazy," said Jack. "I want to sleep."

"You can sleep when we come back home," said Annie. "No time will have passed."

Jack sighed.

But he got out of bed.

"Yes!" whispered Annie. "Meet you at the back door." She tiptoed out of Jack's room.

Jack yawned. He pulled on his jeans and trainers and a sweatshirt. He put his notebook and pencil into his rucksack. Then he crept down the stairs.

Annie opened the back door. Quietly, they stepped outside.

"Wait," said Jack. "We need a torch."

"No, we don't. I told you – the moon will light our way," said Annie. And she set off.

Jack sighed, then followed her.

Annie was right, thought Jack. The moon was so bright that he could see his shadow. Everything seemed washed with silver.

5

Soon they left their street. Annie led the way into the Frog Valley woods. It was much darker under the shadows of the trees.

Jack looked up, searching for the tree house.

"There!" said Annie.

The magic tree house was shining in the moonlight.

Annie grabbed the rope ladder and started climbing up.

"Careful – go slowly," said Jack.

He followed her up the ladder and into the tree house.

Moonlight streamed through the window.

It shone on the letter M that shimmered on the wooden floor.

It shone on the three M things that rested on the M: a *moonstone* from the time of the ninjas, a *mango* from the Amazon rainforest and a *mammoth bone* from the Ice Age.

"We need just one more M thing," said Annie, "to free Morgan from her spell."

Squeak.

"Peanut!" said Annie.

In the dim light, Jack saw a tiny mouse. She sat on an open book.

"You didn't expect to see us this late, did you?" said Annie.

She picked up Peanut. And Jack picked up the open book.

"So where are we going this time?" Annie asked him.

Jack held the book up to the moonlight.

"Uh-oh," he said. "I knew we should have brought a torch. I can't read a thing."

He could make out diagrams and shadowy pictures. But he couldn't read a word.

"Look at the cover," said Annie.

The letters were bigger on the cover. Jack squinted at them.

"It's called *Hello, Moon*," he said.

Annie gasped. "We're going to the moon?"

"Of course not," said Jack. "It's impossible to go to the moon without lots of equipment."

"Why?"

"There's no air. We couldn't breathe. Not only that, we'd boil to death if it was day and freeze to death if it was night."

"Wow," said Annie. "So where do you think we are going?"

"Maybe a place where people train to be astronauts," said Jack.

"That sounds great," said Annie.

"Yes," said Jack. He'd always wanted to meet astronauts and space scientists.

"So say the wish," said Annie.

Jack opened the book again. He pointed to a picture of a dome-shaped structure.

"I wish we could go there," he said.

The wind started to blow.

The tree house started to spin.

It spun faster and faster and faster.

Then everything was silent.

Absolutely silent. As quiet and still as silence could be.

2

Space Hotel

Jack opened his eyes.

He looked out of the window. The tree house had landed inside a large white room.

"What kind of training place is this?" asked Annie.

"I don't know," said Jack.

The room was round. It had no windows. It had a white floor and a curved wall lit by bright lights.

"Hello!" Annie called.

There was no answer.

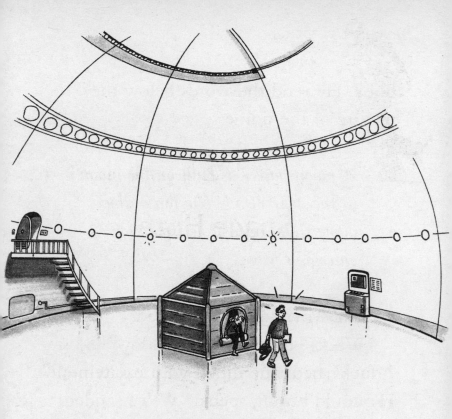

Where were all the astronauts and space scientists? Jack wondered.

"There's nobody here," said Annie.

"How do you know?" said Jack.

"I just feel it," said Annie.

"We'd better find out where we are," said Jack.

He looked at the page in the moon

book. He read the words below the picture of the dome.

A moon base was built on the moon in the year 2031. The top of the dome slides open to let spacecraft enter and leave.

"Oh, wow!" Jack whispered.

"What?" asked Annie.

Jack's heart pounded with excitement. He could hardly speak. "We've landed inside a moon base," he said.

"So . . . ?" said Annie.

"So the moon base is on the moon!" said Jack.

Annie's eyes widened. "We're on the moon?" she asked.

Jack nodded. "The book says the moon base was built in the year 2031," he said.

"So this book was written *after* that! Which means this book is from the *future*!"

"Oh, wow," said Annie. "Morgan must have gone forward in time to borrow it from a future library."

"Exactly," said Jack. "And now we're in the future, on the moon."

Squeak, squeak!

Annie and Jack looked at Peanut. The mouse was running around in circles.

"Poor Peanut," said Annie.

She tried to pick the mouse up. But Peanut hid behind the mango on the letter M.

"Maybe she's nervous about being on the moon," said Annie.

"She's not the only one," said Jack. He let out a deep breath, then he pushed his glasses into place.

"So what's a moon base?" asked Annie.

Jack looked at the book. He read aloud: "*When scientists visit the moon for short periods, they eat and sleep in the moon base.*"

"A space hotel!" said Annie.

"I suppose so," said Jack. He read more: "*The small base has a landing chamber and a room for storing spacesuits. Air and temperature controls make breathing possible.*

"So that's why we can breathe," Jack said.

"Let's explore," said Annie. "We have to find the fourth thing for Morgan."

"No, first we should study this map," said Jack. He pulled out his notebook.

"You study it," said Annie.

Jack copied the map. Then he drew in the tree house.

"OK," he said. He pointed at the X in

his drawing. "We're *here*."

Jack looked up. Annie was gone.

"Oh, no," he said. As usual, she had left without him. Before they could even make a plan.

Jack put the moon book and pencil into his bag. Carrying his notebook and rucksack, he started to climb out of the window.

Squeak! Squeak!

Jack looked back at Peanut. The mouse

15

was running back and forth on the M.

"Stay here and be safe," said Jack. "We'll be back soon."

He swung himself over the windowsill. His feet touched the floor of the landing chamber.

"Annie!" he called.

There was no answer.

Jack looked at his diagram.

It showed only one way to go. Jack walked along the curved white wall to the stairs.

He climbed the steps to a hallway.

"Jack! Hurry!" Annie was at the end of the hallway, standing in the airlock. She peered out of a window in a giant door.

Jack hurried towards her. Annie stepped aside so he could look out of the window too.

"Oh, wow," said Jack. What he saw took his breath away.

He stared at a rocky grey land. The land was filled with giant craters and tall mountains. The sun was shining. But the sky was ink-black!

"Say hi to the moon," Annie said softly.

3

Open Sesame!

"The fourth M thing must be out there," said Annie.

Beside the door was a button with the word OPEN on it. Annie reached for the button.

"Wait!" Jack grabbed her hand. "There's no air on the moon. Remember?"

"Oh, yes. But we have to go out to find the M thing."

"Let's see what the book says," said Jack.

He pulled the book out of his bag. He flipped through it until he found a page that showed the surface of the moon. He read aloud: "*It takes fourteen Earth days to equal one day on the moon. No air protects the moon from the sun's rays, so the daytime heat reaches 260 degrees.*"

Jack looked at Annie. "I told you our blood would boil if we went out there," he said.

"Yuck," she said.

Jack read from the book again: "*Moon scientists wear spacesuits, which have controls to keep them from getting too hot or too cold. They have tanks, which provide air for two hours.*"

"Where can we get spacesuits from?" asked Annie. She looked around then trotted back down the hall. "Maybe there . . . ?"

Jack was studying his map. "Let's try the spacesuit storeroom."

"Don't look at the map," said Annie. "Look at the real room!"

Jack glanced up. Annie was peering through a doorway off the hall.

"There's lots of space stuff in here!" she said.

Jack went to look.

Bulky white suits hung from hangers. Air tanks, helmets, gloves and boots sat in neat rows on shelves.

"Wow, it's like the armour room in a castle," said Jack.

"Yes, with huge armour," said Annie.

"Let's pick out the smallest stuff," said Jack, "The suits can go over our clothes."

Annie found the smallest white suit. And Jack found the next smallest white suit. They stepped into them.

Then Annie locked Jack's air tank into place.

"Thanks," he said. And he did the same for her.

"Thanks," she said.

"Gloves?" said Jack. He and Annie pulled on white gloves.

"Boots?" said Annie. They each pulled

on a pair of huge white boots.

"Helmets?" said Jack. He reached for a helmet.

"Wow, they're quite light," he said. "I thought they'd be like knights' helmets."

Jack and Annie put the helmets on. They locked each other's into place.

"I can't move my head to the right or left," said Annie.

"Me neither," said Jack. "Let's try walking."

Jack and Annie moved clumsily around the room. Jack felt like a fat snowman.

"Close your visor," said Annie.

They both closed their see-through visors. Cool air filled Jack's helmet.

"I CAN BREATHE!" Annie yelled. Her voice boomed in Jack's ears.

"Ow! Talk quietly," Jack said. "We have two-way radios inside our helmets."

"Sorry," whispered Annie.

Jack put the moon book back in his bag. Then he slung the bag over his shoulder.

"OK!" he said. "Remember, we only have two hours of air in our tanks. So we need to find the fourth M thing really quickly."

"I hope we can find it," said Annie.

"Me too," said Jack. He knew they

could not go home until they did.

"Let's go," said Annie. She gave Jack a little push.

"Careful. Don't mess around," he said. "We don't want to fall over in these suits."

"Just go. Go!" said Annie. She pushed him out of the room. They walked back to the airlock.

"Are you ready?" said Annie. "Open sesame!" She pressed the OPEN button. A door slowly slid closed behind them. A door opened in front of them.

And Jack and Annie stepped out onto the moon.

4

Moon Rabbits

"Oh, wow!" said Annie. She took a step forward.

But Jack stood frozen. He wanted to get a good look at everything first.

He stared at the ground. He was standing in a layer of grey dust as fine as powder.

Footprints were everywhere. Jack wondered who had made them.

He reached into his bag for the moon book. To his surprise, it was as light as a feather!

He found a picture of footprints on the moon. He read:

The moon has no rain or wind to blow the dust around. So footprints will never wear away naturally, not even in a billion years.

"Oh, wow," Jack said.

The moon was the stillest place he had ever, ever been. It was as still as a picture. And its stillness would never, ever end.

Jack stared at the ink-black sky. A lovely blue-and-white ball was glowing in the distance.

Earth.

For the first time, it really hit Jack. They were in outer space!

"Look!" Annie cried, laughing.

She bounced past Jack – almost flying

through the
air. She
landed on
her feet.
Then she
jumped again.
"I'm a moon rabbit," she
called.

Jack laughed. *How does she
do that?* he wondered. He
turned a page and read:

*A person weighs less on the moon
because of the moon's low gravity
and lack of air. If you weigh 60
kilos on Earth, you would only
weigh 10 kilos on the moon.*

"Don't just stand there reading!" said
Annie, grabbing the book from Jack's

gloved hand. She threw it into space.

It flew far away.

Jack started to go after it.

He bounced up and down. *Boing! Boing! Boing!* Now *he* felt as light as a feather.

"Look!" he called to Annie. "I'm a moon rabbit too."

Where Jack's boots hit the ground, moondust gracefully sprayed into space.

The book had landed at the edge of a shallow crater.

When Jack reached it, he tried to stop. But his feet slipped.

He fell over and lay on his side. He tried to stand. But he was unbalanced.

He tried again. But the dust was just too deep. And he was too clumsy in his spacesuit.

"Are you OK?" asked Annie.

"I can't get up," said Jack.

"You shouldn't have been messing around," said Annie wisely.

"You messed around first," said Jack. "Now, help me up, please."

Annie started to move towards him.

"Don't fall too," warned Jack.

"I won't." Annie moved very slowly. She half floated, half walked.

"Give me your hand," she said.

Annie grabbed Jack's hand. She pressed her boot against his and pulled him up.

"Thanks," he said.

"It was easy," she said. "You were really light."

"Thank goodness," said Jack. "It's impossible to get up alone."

He picked up the moon book. It was covered in dust. He brushed it off.

"Oh, wow! Look!" said Annie. She stood at the edge of the crater.

"What is it?" said Jack.

"A moon buggy!" said Annie.

The buggy was parked in the crater. It had four huge wheels.

"Let's go for a ride," said Annie.

"We can't," said Jack. "We only have two hours of air in our tanks. Remember?"

"I bet we'll find the M thing faster if we go in the moon buggy!" Annie bounced into the crater.

"But we can't drive!" said Jack.

"I bet I can drive *this*," said Annie. "It looks easy. Come on!"

She jumped into the driver's seat.

"But you don't have a driving licence!" said Jack.

"Who cares?" said Annie. "There aren't any roads on the moon, or traffic lights, or policemen either."

She was right, Jack thought.

"Well, go slowly," he said. And he climbed in beside her.

Annie pushed a button labelled ON.

The moon buggy lurched backwards.

"Uh-oh!" said Annie.

"Put on the brake!" said Jack.

Annie pressed a pedal on the floor. The buggy stopped with a jerk.

"Phew," she said.

"It must be in reverse," said Jack. "Let

me have a look—"

But before he could look at anything,
Annie pushed another button.

The buggy tilted back. Its
front wheels started to rise
into the air.

"Let me out of here!" said Jack.

Annie pushed more buttons.

The buggy's front wheels landed back
on the ground. And the buggy leaped
forward.

"*Slower!*" said Jack.

"I can't," said Annie. "I don't know how!"

Annie steered the buggy over the tracks on the ground. The wide wheels kept it from sinking into the deep dust.

"Careful!" said Jack.

The buggy zoomed out of the crater.

Grey clouds of dust rose behind them as they set off across the moon.

5

Hang On!

Annie drove the moon buggy over bumps and hollows.

"I'm going through *there*!" She pointed to an opening between two mountains.

Jack held onto the dashboard.

The buggy bumped towards the opening and shot through it.

On the other side, the ground was even rockier.

"Look for the f-fourth M thing!" said Annie, bouncing up and down.

Jack groaned. Looking for anything on

this wild ride was impossible.

"Sl-slow d-down!" he said.

"How?"

"Try pressing on the b-brake pedal. On the f-floor. Slowly!"

Annie pressed on the brake.

The buggy slowed down. Jack sighed with relief. The ride was still bumpy. But now, at least, he could take a good look at the moon.

He had never been to such a colourless, barren place. There was no green, no blue, no red.

No water, no trees, no clouds.

Only giant grey rocks and craters – and an American flag.

"Oh, wow," said Jack. "That's from the first astronauts who landed on the moon!"

"And look – a telescope!" said Annie.

She drove up to the flag. Then she put her foot on the brake until the buggy stopped.

She pressed a button that said OFF. Then she and Jack hopped out.

They took slow giant steps to the site of the first moon landing.

Beside the flag was a sign. Annie read it:

HERE MEN FROM THE PLANET EARTH
FIRST SET FOOT UPON THE MOON,
JULY 1969 A.D.
WE CAME IN PEACE
FOR ALL MANKIND.

"That's a good message," said Jack.

He handed the moon book to Annie.
Then he took out his notebook and
pencil to copy the sign.

"Let's leave our own message," said
Annie.

"What would we
say?" said Jack.

"The same thing," said Annie. "But say we are the first children."

Jack turned to a new page in his notebook. In big letters he wrote their message.

"Now we have to sign it," Annie said.

Jack signed his name.

Then he passed the notebook and pencil to Annie. She signed her name and passed the notebook back.

Jack tore out the piece of paper. He put it by the flag.

Today the first kids from the planet Earth came to the Moon. We came in peace for all children.
Jack
ANNIE

No wind would ever blow the message away. No rain would ever fall on it.

It would be there for ever, unless someone moved it.

Thinking of "for ever" made Jack feel dizzy. He shook his head to clear his thoughts. Then he remembered the time. Had two hours passed yet?

"I wish I had a watch," he said, standing up. "We might be running out of time."

"Oh, wow. A moon man!" said Annie.

"What?" Jack turned to look at her.

She was staring through the telescope.

Jack walked over to the telescope. Annie stepped aside so he could look too.

Jack gasped. In the distance, something was flying above the ground.

It looked like a giant man in a spacesuit.

41

6

High Jump

"Who is *that*?" said Jack.

"I don't know," said Annie. "But we'll soon find out!" She started waving.

"No!" said Jack. He grabbed her arm. "Let's go back to the base – before he gets here!"

"Why?" said Annie.

"We don't know who he is!" said Jack. "We don't know if he's friendly or not."

"But we can't go back," said Annie. "We haven't found the fourth M thing yet. We won't be able to go home."

"It doesn't matter. We can lock the door at the moon base until he goes away," said Jack. "Then we can get new air tanks!"

Jack hurried to the moon buggy. "Come on!" He jumped into the driver's seat.

Annie gave a little wave. Then she climbed into the moon buggy. The buggy set off.

"Careful!" said Annie.

They bumped over the rocks as Jack turned the buggy round. Then they zoomed towards the pass.

Jack steered around craters and rocks. More than once the buggy nearly tipped over.

"Whoa! Slow down!" said Annie.

They were almost at the mountain pass. Suddenly, a cloud of dust flew up in front of them. The ground trembled.

"Watch it!" cried Annie.

Jack couldn't see a thing.

He put on the brake. The buggy jerked to a stop.

The dust settled.

A giant rock had fallen into the narrow pass. It was stuck between two walls of rock. They were trapped!

Jack quickly found a picture of a

giant rock in the moon book. He read
aloud: "*Rocks of all sizes crash into the
moon from outer space. These rocks are
called meteorites.*

"We're lucky that meteorite didn't
land on us," said Jack.

"Yes, and I suppose it's too big to
be the M thing," said Annie. She
had climbed out of the moon buggy

and was standing by the meteorite.

It was more than twice as tall as she was.

Jack looked at the black sky. The flying thing was nowhere in sight – yet.

"We'll have to jump over it," Annie said.

"Jump? I don't think so," said Jack. "It's too high."

"I'm going to try anyway," said Annie.
"Wait. Let's think first," said Jack.
But Annie was already backing up.
"One, two, three – go!" she shouted,
and took giant, leaping steps towards
the meteorite.
When Annie got close to the rock,
she pushed off the ground. Then she flew
through space and disappeared behind
the meteorite.
"Annie!' Jack called.
There was no answer.
"Oh, no," Jack said. He backed
up and set off towards the rock.
He jumped as high as he
could. Then he was flying
through space.
Jack hit the ground and fell
face down in the dust.
He tried to stand up. But his

suit was too bulky. He tried to roll over.
But his suit made even that impossible.

"Oh, no," he groaned. "Not again."

"Are you here?" asked Annie. "Did you
make it?"

"Yes!" Jack was relieved to hear her
voice. But he couldn't turn his head to
see her. He could only hear her over the
radio.

"Can you help me up?" he asked.

"No," said Annie.

"Why not?"

"I fell over too," she said.

"Oh, no," Jack sighed. "Now we are
really in trouble."

He tried to stand up again. And failed.

"Can you see anything?" he asked.

"Just the sky," said Annie. "Wow, it's
weird . . ."

"I'm worried about our air tanks," said

Jack. "I feel like it's been two hours."

"Ja–ack . . ." said Annie.

"And what about that moon man?" said Jack. "Where's he gone?"

"Jack!" whispered Annie.

"What?"

"He's here," she said. "The moon man is here."

"*What?*"

"He's standing above me."

7

The Moon Man

Jack's heart nearly stopped beating.

He could hear Annie talking.

"Hi," she said. "We come in peace."

There was silence. Then Jack heard Annie say, "Thank you. I have to help my brother up now."

A moment later, Annie rolled Jack onto his back.

She grabbed his hand and pulled him up.

"Thanks," said Jack, once he was standing.

The moon man was a few metres away. His face was hidden by a metal visor.

He looked like a spaceman. A huge spaceman – with a giant tank on his back. It was as big as a refrigerator.

"That's a jet pack!" said Jack. "I've seen pictures of future astronauts flying with those things. It's like a mini-spaceship. Isn't it?"

The moon man didn't answer.

"I don't think he can hear us," said Annie. "He's not hooked up to our radio."

"Oh," said Jack. "I'll write him a message!"

"Good idea," said Annie.

Jack pulled out his notebook and pencil. He wrote:

We're Jack and Annie.
We come in peace from
America. Who are you?

Jack handed the notebook and his pencil to the moon man. They looked tiny in his big hands.

The moon man looked down at the message. He looked at the tiny pencil. Then he turned the notebook over.

Jack and Annie watched as the moon man put the pencil to the paper. He was writing something very carefully.

Finally he gave the notebook back to Jack.

Jack and Annie stared at the marks.

"Stars," said Annie. "He's drawn stars."

"Maybe it's a space map," said Jack.

"Space map?" said Annie. "Hey, Jack, *map* starts with M!"

"Oh, wow," said Jack. "This must be the fourth M thing!"

"Let's ask him what his map means," said Annie. She turned round.

"We'll never know now," she said.

"Why?" Jack looked up from the map.

"That's why." Annie pointed. The moon man was flying over the mountains.

"Thanks!" she cried.

8

One Star to Another

"Who *was* that man?" said Jack. "What does his map mean?"

"I don't know," said Annie. "But let's see if it works."

Jack took a deep breath. "Yes, we'd better hurry back. I think I'm running out of air. It feels harder to breathe."

"Me too," said Annie.

"Go slowly. Don't breathe too deeply," said Jack.

He and Annie took long, floating steps towards the moon base. Jack held his breath as if he were underwater.

By the time they got to the white dome, he was ready to burst.

Annie pushed a button beside the huge door. It slid open. They hurried into the airlock. The door closed behind them and the door to the hallway opened.

Jack opened the visor of his helmet. He took a long, deep breath – and let it out. "Ahhhh!"

"Let's get out of these suits," said Annie.

"Good idea." Jack was dying to free his arms and legs.

As they moved clumsily into the space-suit storeroom, Jack felt heavy again.

He and Annie unlocked each other's helmets, gloves and boots, and pulled everything off. Then they stepped out of their bulky suits.

"Phew!" Jack said. He took off his glasses and rubbed his eyes.

It was great to be free – even if he no longer felt as light as a feather.

"Hurry! Peanut's waiting!" said Annie.

She led the way down the steps to the bright landing chamber.

"Yes," she said softly.

Jack was relieved to see the tree house still there. Soon they'd be heading home. He couldn't wait.

Jack and Annie crawled through the tree-house window.

"We're back,
Peanut!" said Annie.

Squeak! Peanut
ran to the letter M.

"We missed you!"
said Annie. She patted the mouse's head.
"We met a moon man."

"Sorry, Peanut, but you have to move,"
said Jack. "We have to put the map on
the M."

Annie gently lifted the mouse off the
M.

Jack tore the star map out of his
notebook. He placed it on the M, with
the mammoth bone, the mango and the
moonstone.

He sighed, then sat back on his heels.
"Hand me the Frog Valley book," he
said. They needed the Frog Valley book
to get back home.

There was silence.

Jack turned and looked at Annie.

"It's not working, Jack," she said. "The book's not here."

"What?" Was the map the wrong thing?

They looked around the tree house.

"It's definitely not here," said Annie.

"Oh, no." Jack's heart sank. He picked up the star map and stared at it.

Squeak, squeak. Peanut jumped out of Annie's arms and scurried back to the letter M.

"I've got an idea," said Jack. He reached into his bag and took out his pencil.

"What are you doing?" said Annie.

"Do you know how you draw a constellation?" said Jack. "You connect all the stars. What will happen if we try that?"

He drew a line
from one star to
another. He kept drawing, until all the
stars were connected.

"Let me see," said Annie.

Jack held the paper out so they could
both study it.

"It looks like a mouse," said Annie.

"Yes," said Jack.

"Is there such a thing as a mouse
constellation?" she Annie.

"I don't think so . . ." said Jack.

Squeak.

Annie and Jack looked at Peanut. She
was standing on the M.

"Oh, wow. Jack," Annie whispered, "I
think I know what the fourth thing is."

Jack grinned. "Me too," he said. "It's
a—"

"*Mouse!*" they said together.

Squeak! Squeak!

"Maybe the spell is *Moonstone, mango, mammoth bone, mouse!*" said Annie.

Jack touched each M thing in turn as he whispered, "Moonstone, mango, mammoth bone, mouse."

"Let's say it over and over and see what happens," said Annie.

Together, they chanted:

"*Moonstone, mango,*
mammoth bone, mouse.
Moonstone, mango,
mammoth bone, mouse."

Suddenly, a bright light filled the tree house.

The light got brighter and brighter and brighter.

The brightness was blinding and whirling.

The air spun with brightness.

Then everything was clear.

Peanut the mouse was gone.

And Morgan le Fay stood before Jack and Annie.

9

Morgan

"Thank you," Morgan said softly. "You have freed me from the magician's spell."

Jack just stared at her.

"*You* were Peanut?" Annie said.

Morgan nodded and smiled.

"Really? You were with us all the time?" said Jack. "On all our missions?"

Morgan nodded again.

"Why did we have to go on this mission to find a mouse," said Jack, "if you were always with us?"

"To break the spell we had to be on

the moon,"
said Morgan.
"You could
have
broken it
the minute
we arrived."

"Oh, that's
what Peanut — I mean *you* were trying to
say!" said Annie. "We didn't have to leave
the moon base at all."

Morgan nodded, smiling.

"But the moon man came along to
help us," said Annie. "He drew a
constellation of a mouse! Is he a friend
of yours?"

Morgan shrugged. "Let's just say we
had a little talk. He came to the moon
base while you were out."

"The same way you had a talk with

the ninja master?" said Jack. "And the monkey and the sorcerer?"

Morgan nodded. "I always squeaked to the ones who helped you."

"But how did they understand you as a mouse?" said Jack.

Morgan smiled again. "Certain wise ones understand the language of little creatures," she said.

"I bet it was you who turned the pages of the books!" said Annie. "To show us where to go next!"

Morgan nodded.

"But who turned you into a mouse?" said Annie.

Morgan frowned. "A certain person who likes to play tricks on me," she said. "His name is Merlin."

"Merlin!" said Jack. "The greatest magician who ever lived."

Morgan sniffed. "He's not that great," she said. "He doesn't even know I have two brave friends who help me."

"Us?" said Annie shyly.

Morgan nodded. "And I thank you both with all my heart."

"You're welcome," said Jack and Annie.

Morgan handed Annie the Frog Valley book. "Are you ready to go home now?" she asked.

"Yes!" said Jack and Annie.

Annie pointed to a picture of the Frog Valley woods. "I wish we could go there," she said.

The tree house started to spin.

It spun faster and faster and faster.

Then everything was still.

Absolutely still.

But only for a moment.

10

Earth Life

The midnight woods woke up.

A breeze rustled the leaves.

An owl hooted.

The sounds were soft, but very alive.

Jack opened his eyes. He pushed his glasses into place.

He smiled. Morgan was still with them. He could see her in the moonlight. Her long white hair was shining.

"Morgan, can you and the tree house stay here?" said Annie. "In Frog Valley?"

"No, I must leave again, I'm afraid,"

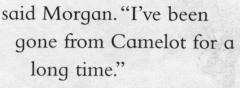

said Morgan. "I've been gone from Camelot for a long time."

She handed Jack his bag. She brushed his cheek. Her hand felt soft and cool.

"There's a bit of moondust still on you," she said. "Thank you, Jack, for your great love of knowledge."

"You're welcome," said Jack.

Morgan tugged one of Annie's braids. "And thank you, Annie, for your belief in the impossible."

"You're welcome," said Annie.

"Go home now," said Morgan.

Jack smiled. Home was Earth – that bright, colourful world where everything was alive and always changing.

"Bye, Morgan," said Annie. She started

to climb
down
from the
tree house.
Jack looked
at Morgan.
"Will you come
back soon?" he said.

"Anything can happen," said Morgan.
"The universe is filled with wonders.
Isn't it, Jack?"

He smiled and nodded.

"Go now," Morgan said softly.

Jack followed Annie down the rope
ladder. He stepped onto the ground.

The wind started to blow.

The tree started to shake.

A loud roar filled Jack's ears. He
squeezed his eyes shut. He covered
his ears.

Then everything was silent and still.

Jack opened his eyes. The ladder was gone. He looked through the leaves and branches of the giant oak tree. Where the tree house had been there was only moonlight now.

"Bye, Morgan," he whispered sadly.

"Bye, Peanut," said Annie.

Jack and Annie stared at the top of the tree for a long moment.

"Ready?" said Annie.

Jack nodded.

They set off home.

The midnight air felt cool and moist. It was filled with the soft sounds of earth life.

Jack and Annie left the Frog Valley woods. They started down their street.

Annie glanced up at the sky. "The moon looks really far away, doesn't it!"

It did, thought Jack. It *was*.

"I wonder how the moon man can be up there all alone," said Annie.

"What do you mean?" said Jack.

"I mean, who helps him put on his spacesuit?" said Annie. "Who helps him get up when he falls over?"

"And who is he?" added Jack.

"Who do you think he was?" said Annie.

"He must be a scientist or an astronaut from Earth," said Jack.

"No. I think he's an alien," said Annie, "from another galaxy."

Jack scoffed. "What makes you say that?"

"I just feel it," said Annie.

"Wrong," said Jack. "There's no proof that aliens exist."

"Maybe not now," said Annie. "But

don't forget — we were in the future."

They crossed their garden and climbed their back steps. Annie tiptoed inside the house. Jack followed her.

Before he shut the door, he glanced up at the moon.

Was Annie right? he wondered. Could the moon man have come from another galaxy?

Morgan's words came back to him: *The universe is filled with wonders. Isn't it, Jack?*

"Goodnight, moon man," Jack whispered. Then he closed the door.